Now Cow Helps Fighter Spider

A Mindful Tale for Coping with Anger

by Kelly Caleb

Illustrations by

John Van Hout III

Visit our website at NowCowBooks.com
Facebook Page: Now Cow Books, Inc.
Facebook Group: Now Cow Mindful Readers
Instagram: nowcowdramallama
Twitter @nowcowdramalla1

Library of Congress Control Number: 2020923442
ISBN: 978-1-7333783-2-1

Now Cow Helps Fighter Spider: A Mindful Tale for Coping with Anger
Written by Kelly Caleb
Illustrations by John Van Hout III - 1st edition, Book 4 of the Now Cow Series

Also read:
Now Cow Helps Drama Llama: A Mindful Tale for Coping with Anxiety
Now Cow Helps Bad Habit Rabbit: A Mindful Tale for Changing Behaviors
Now Cow Helps Lost My Shoe Caribou: A Mindful Tale for Personal Responsibility

Dedication

This book is dedicated to every child who struggles with managing anger and other negative emotions.

Special thanks to Elise, Ross, Fox, and Seph Erickson. Elise, I appreciate all your hard work editing and completing the graphic design. Ross, thank you for the encouragement. Fox and Seph, thank you for being excited about Now Cow, Drama Llama, Bad Habit Rabbit, and waiting so patiently for Fighter Spider to be done, and also for sharing your mommy so she could help me publish this book.

This book (and all the Now Cow Books) would not be possible without the support and encouragement of the Martin Family. Thank you Liz, Paul, Cole, and Emily, extra thanks to Brooklyn and Piper.

As always, to honor the memory of Jack Cole Martin and assist children and adolescents with the challenges of mental health (and particularly to fight against issues of bullying and suicide by educating and promoting acceptance, belonging, and positive actions that lead to good choices), 10% of all profits from the Now Cow Book series are donated to operationjacksvillage at https://operationjacksvillage.org/.

#operationjacksvillage
#istandwithjack

1

Fighter Spider got her name
from acting tough instead of tame.

She liked to fight with all eight fists,
she'd jump and kick with spinning twists.

If a brown twig snapped or cracked,
fighter Spider would react.

She'd hop and yell and look about
hoping for something to clout.

But often there was nothing there,
just Fighter Spider punching air

She frightened all the little bugs
when they crawled across the rugs

in search of food or bug playthings,
causing them to flap their wings

and cry out in distress and fear.
They all learned to stay quite clear
of Fighter Spider's web and nest
to avoid undue distress.

So Fighter Spider was alone,
no calls on the telephone.

Her mom and dad just shook their heads
and made her practice weaving threads

to spin her web to catch some food
and maybe find a better mood.

Fighter Spider got kicked out of school
because she broke the peaceful rule.

And she had no self-control
when she played sports and scored a goal.

She taunted all the other players.
Once she tied them up in layers
of spider silk that got them sticky
and left them all feeling quite icky.

No one wanted her around
both in the air and on the ground.
Which made her want to fight some more
so she could even up the score.

But there was no one left to fight
and there was no one left to bite.

So she crawled the forest floor alone
with an angry spiteful groan.

Spider's groan was overheard
by gentle Now Cow who preferred
a peaceful, calm and pleasant talk
when she went for her daily walk.

So she spoke up to Fighter Spider
and offered to walk on beside her.

Fighter Spider heard the word
and quicker than a hummingbird

pounced at Now Cow in attack
and tried to give Now Cow a smack.

Now Cow blinked and stepped aside
for she took it all in stride.
But Fighter Spider tried again,
pouncing to disturb the Zen

of Now Cow with a whack and punch.
But Now Cow calmly chewed her lunch
and evaded every chop
with a sideways peaceful hop

Fighter Spider tried once more
to see if she could land a score.

She zoomed by Now Cow on a thread
and tried to bite her on the head.
Now Cow evaded all attacks,
all the swatting jolting thwacks,

leaving Fighter Spider quite surprised
and not a little tantalized.
For no one else had yet evaded
her attacks and she felt quite deflated.

Fighter Spider had to ask
"Now Cow, how do you wear a mask

of peacefulness but fight so well?
I want the 411 intel".

Now Cow mooed, "I did not fight,
I simply evaded your kick and bite.
My peacefulness is not a mask,
it is a daily search and task.

Within my soul I look for peace
and with my peace I get release
from anger and from sorrow too.
That's something I can offer you,

if you would like to learn some skills
and find quiet tranquil thrills."

Fighter Spider made a face.
"But where's the fight? The charge? The race?

How will people know I'm tough?
How will I keep my muscles buff?"

Now Cow said, "Come on Dear Spider"
and Fighter Spider walked beside her.
Now Cow said, "You are confused.
Your self-restraint is underused.

First breathe in and then breathe out
before you jump around and shout.
For fighting does not make you tough,
violence only makes you rough.

Strength arises from within.
Think about your Yang and Yin.
You need balance in your life
or your days will end in strife".

Fighter Spider muttered complaint
about the concept of restraint.
But she thought about her days
and her fighting yelling ways.

And realized she had no friends
and wanted to have better ends

She saw Now Cow's control and power
and figured if she spent an hour,
she might get that skill set too.
So she listened to the moo

of Now Cow's words and hard advice.
She listened once and listened twice.

Every day she learned to sit,
and often while she spun and knit
her web she wrote out the advice.
And she slowly paid the price

of learning to breathe in and out.
To use soft words instead of shout.

She got a journal and she wrote
thoughts and often times she'd quote
wisdom from a book she read
that fed her soul and filled her head.

Slowly over time she changed,
her priorities were rearranged.

Writer Spider got her name
from the quotes that she'd proclaim.
She liked to write with all eight claws
and found this helped correct her flaws.

If a brown twig snapped or cracked,
Writer Spider watched and tracked.
She'd stop and listen and look about,
trying hard to check it out.

But often there was nothing there,
just Writer Spider breathing air.

She apologized to all the little bugs
when they crawled across the rugs,
in search of food or bug playthings.
They no longer flapped their wings

or cried out in distress and fear.
They learned that she would lend an ear
and listen to their little woes
and write them some insightful prose.

Writer Spider was no more alone,
she got calls by telephone.

Her mom and dad were very proud
and they often said aloud,
"We think that you should keep on writing.
It's better for you than the fighting."

Fighter Spider went to school
and learned to follow every rule.

She discovered self-control
when she played sports and scored a goal.

She learned to be part of a team
and learned it was a better dream
to help the whole team win as one
and focus on just having fun.

Teammates wanted her around
both in the air and on the ground.
Which made her want to play some more
so she could help the others score.

45   Sometimes she still wanted to fight,
and sometimes she thought she might bite.
So she would spend some time alone
and let out her angry goan.

She spun a silky web thread sack
that she could punch and give a whack.

And sometimes she went for a walk
with Now Cow so that they could talk.
And sometimes the two friends would spar,
though the sight was quite bizarre.

But always first they'd meditate
to keep their minds and focus straight.

Spider grew in all her skills
and found quiet tranquil thrills.

She got a journal and she wrote
thoughts and often times she'd quote

wisdom from a book she read
that fed her soul and filled her head.

Writer Spider would push and pull,
threads until her web was full
of strength she gathered from within,
she thought about her Yang and Yin.

She learned to live within the Now.
A lesson she learned from a cow
who cared enough to help a friend
find peace, and help her soul transcend.

And if there's a fighter inside you,
take a lesson from these two.

First breathe in and then breathe out,
talk a lot and walk about.
Gather your strength from within,
and balance out your Yang and Yin.

Made in the USA
Las Vegas, NV
08 April 2022

46891598R10036